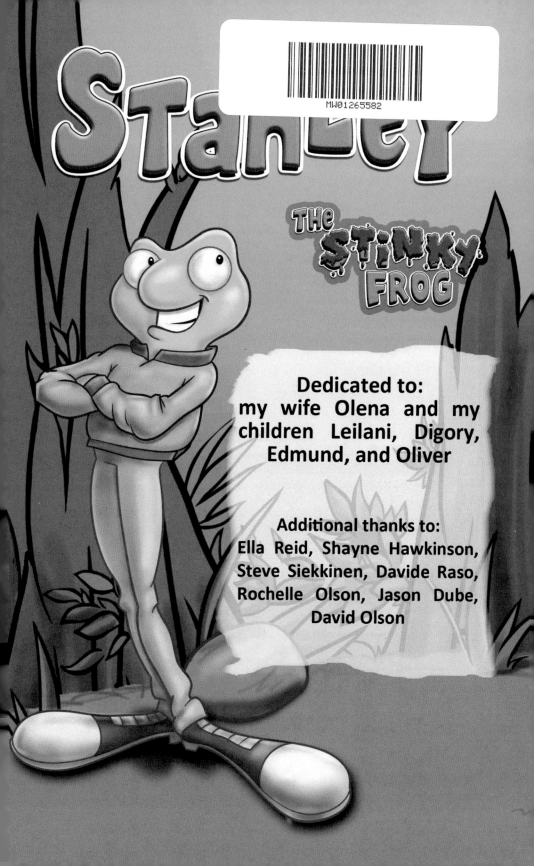

Stanley

THE STINKY FROG

Dedicated to:
my wife Olena and my
children Leilani, Digory,
Edmund, and Oliver

Additional thanks to:
Ella Reid, Shayne Hawkinson,
Steve Siekkinen, Davide Raso,
Rochelle Olson, Jason Dube,
David Olson

On the outskirts of Frogtown, just past the intersection of Lilypad Lane and Boggy Boulevard, there lived a frog named Stanley.

Now, I don't need to tell you about Frogtown. Any amphibian knows that it's simply THE place for the finest, fanciest frogs. It's where singer Jerry Croaker lives, and Buddy 'Legs' Leaper, who once jumped across an entire sidewalk in a single hop. And don't forget Leroy Licker, whose tongue stretches halfway to the sky - or so his legend goes.

But Stanley wasn't one of those - he was just the 187th of Merle and Gloria Frog's 483 tadpoles. He liked sitting on logs in the day and croaking in the reeds at night. No, there was nothing special about Stanley.

Well, except maybe one thing.

Stanley LOVED to eat flies.

You're probably thinking that isn't so special. After all, ALL frogs love to eat flies! It's as plain as the green on their noses. But Stanley REALLY loved flies, any kind he could get! Big, fat juicy ones. Little bizzy buzzy ones. Green ones, fuzzy ones, black ones, crunchy ones. Houseflies, fruit flies and bluebottles. Except, of course, for horseflies, but that's a story for another time.

That's why on this beautiful sunny morning, Stanley made himself plop out of bed (when he really would have liked to sleep in) and wash his face and hands (when he really wanted to sit in the mud) and try for the thousandth time to figure out what to do with his toothbrush and comb.

Because like all good frogs, he never forgot what his teachers at Little Pond Elementary said long ago: Time's fun when you're having flies!

His first stop was Slimy Swamp, or as Stanley liked to call it, the Eat-til-you-Croak Fly Buffet. But on this busy morning he had to push and push to even get into line.

He was almost up to the fruit fly salad when a group of big frogs ran into him from behind, making him drop his plate and sending him sprawling on the mossy ground.

"Make way, tadpole," said one of them. "Big frog coming through!" And who was in the middle of the crowd but Jerry Croaker himself!

Jerry smiled and waved to all his fans while his toadies grabbed fistfuls of flies. He blew kisses as they snatched up every last wing. And he left to eat his breakfast without so much as saying sorry to poor Stanley!

"I guess if you're famous, you get the flies," harrumphed Stanley, but he didn't like it one bit. He decided to head to the Buzz Off Diner in the middle of Frogtown.

As he hopped, Stanley dreamed about
delicious deep-dish pizza flies, and
flyburgers with french flies, and maybe
some crispy gnatcorn. But when he got
to the diner, the line was out the door!

Stanley was so hungry that he waited and waited. When he finally sat down, he saw why the wait was so long. The cooks were making plates very quickly, but none of them were getting to the tables! At the counter sat Leroy Licker, with a glass of frosty bug juice. Every time a tray of flies walked by - ZAP!

Leroy would shoot out his lightning quick tongue and gobble it down before anyone knew what happened!

Needless to say, Stanley was too hungry to wait for Leroy to fill up. "I wish I had a tongue like that!" thought Stanley.

But wishing and having are two different things, even for frogs, so Stanley headed to Mud Hill, where his sometimes-friend Georgie likes to go, to get some fresh flies.

Mud Hill flies, of course, are stringy and taste like cotton candy - which sounds OK to you and me, but to a frog, that's what a moldy hair cake with earwax frosting would be to us. Still, Stanley was STARVING!

When he got to Mud Hill, even the yucky flies were hard to catch. They kept buzzing and bizzing and bazzing just out of reach. In fact, only one frog was filling up at Mud Hill - Legs Leaper. He would sit verrrry still for a verrry long time, waiting for a fly to settle down almost 20 whole inches away, and then SPROINNNNGGG! He would jump and snatch it out of the air, as neat as can be.

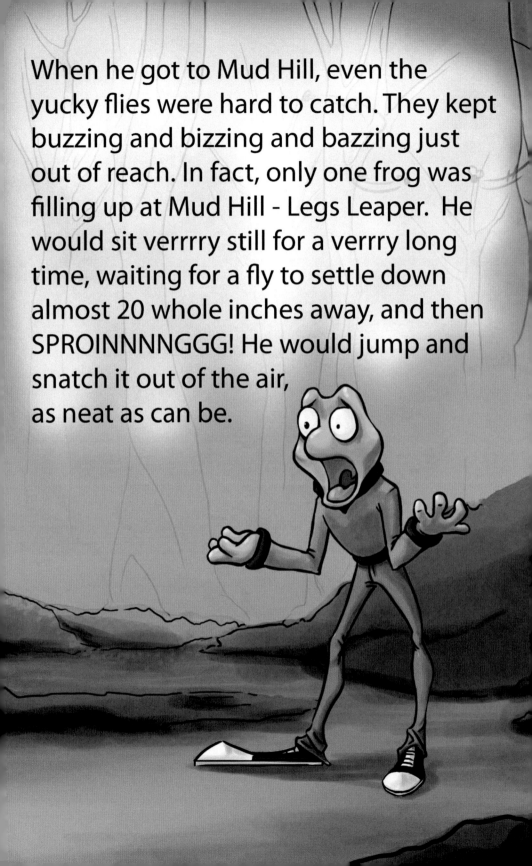

Stanley tried that trick, but all he ever got out of it was a mouthful of mud and an earful of teasing from the flies. "Silly Stanley can't catch us!" they buzzed.

"If I could jump farther you wouldn't laugh at me," he huffed. He was right, but he still couldn't jump farther.

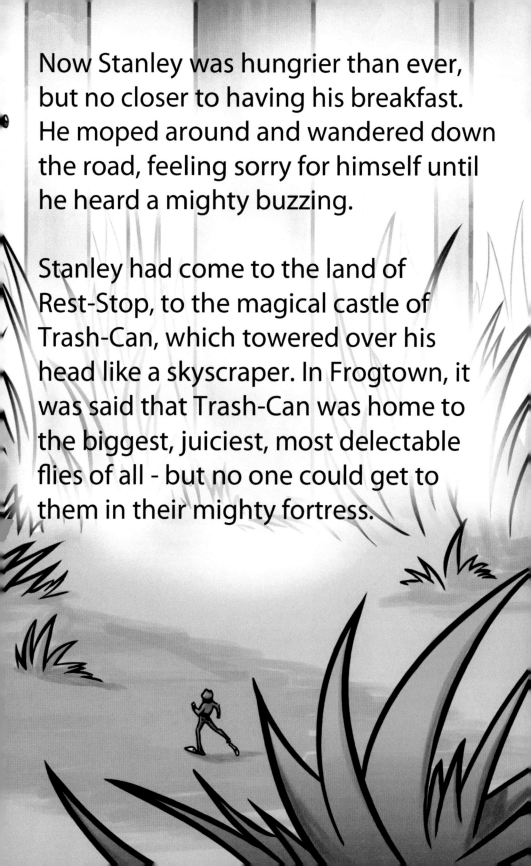

Now Stanley was hungrier than ever, but no closer to having his breakfast. He moped around and wandered down the road, feeling sorry for himself until he heard a mighty buzzing.

Stanley had come to the land of Rest-Stop, to the magical castle of Trash-Can, which towered over his head like a skyscraper. In Frogtown, it was said that Trash-Can was home to the biggest, juiciest, most delectable flies of all - but no one could get to them in their mighty fortress.

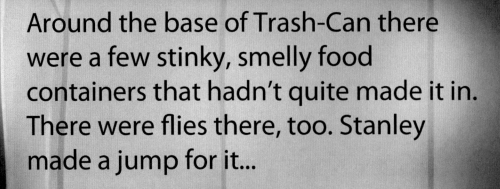

Around the base of Trash-Can there were a few stinky, smelly food containers that hadn't quite made it in. There were flies there, too. Stanley made a jump for it...

...and THUD! He crashed into the ground while the flies scattered and spiraled up to the top, their buzzy laughter trickling down behind them. "Why can't I be special," cried Stanley.

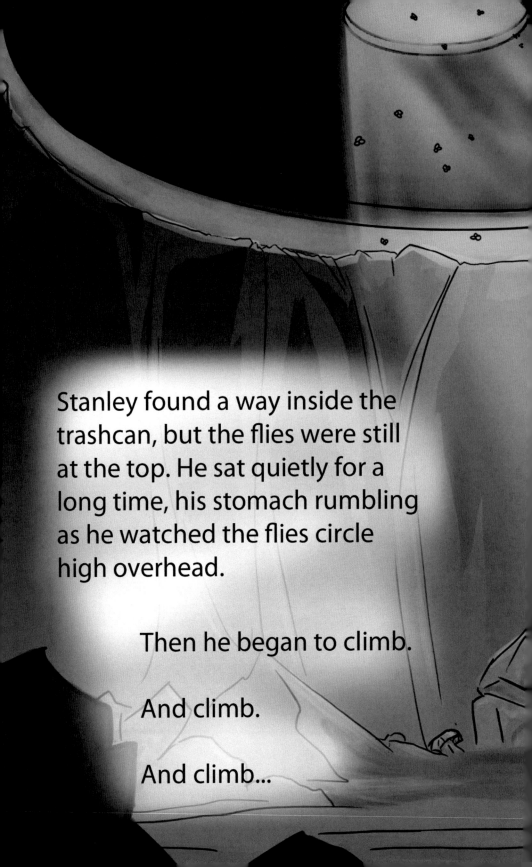

Stanley found a way inside the trashcan, but the flies were still at the top. He sat quietly for a long time, his stomach rumbling as he watched the flies circle high overhead.

Then he began to climb.

And climb.

And climb...

He climbed almost all the way up, which was pretty amazing for a frog of the non-tree-frog variety. When he was just below the top, he began to get excited. A few more inches and he'd be at the top, surrounded by flies.

"I did it!" he croaked happily to himself. And he got ready to jump...

...and lost his grip! Down he fell...

...down...

...down...

...and SPLAT! Right into the stinky carton of week-old Chinese take-out. He fell so hard he broke right through the crusty top and into the ooze beneath!

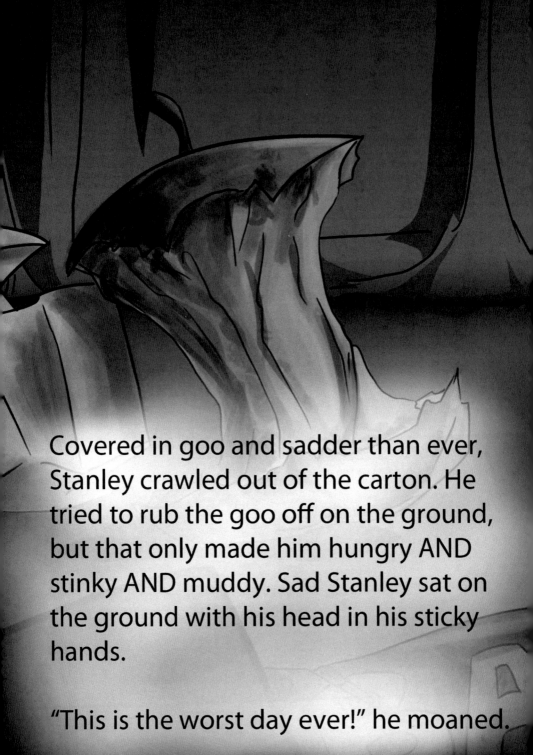

Covered in goo and sadder than ever, Stanley crawled out of the carton. He tried to rub the goo off on the ground, but that only made him hungry AND stinky AND muddy. Sad Stanley sat on the ground with his head in his sticky hands.

"This is the worst day ever!" he moaned.

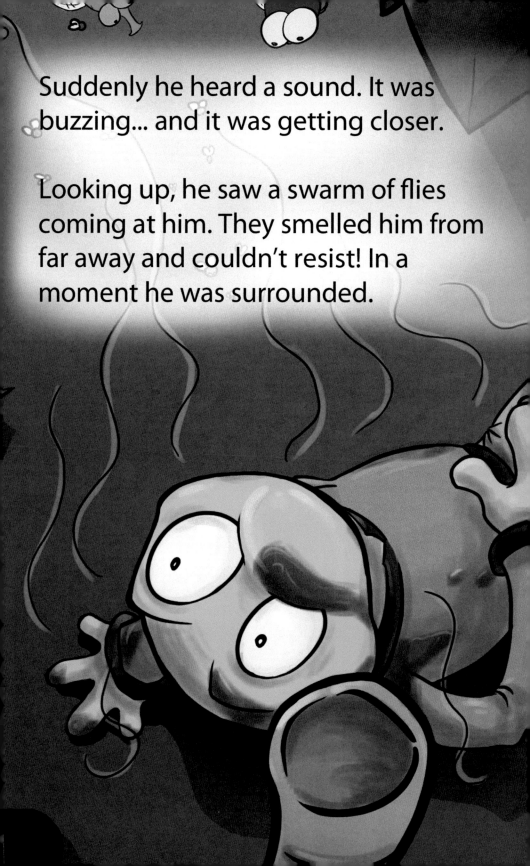

Suddenly he heard a sound. It was buzzing... and it was getting closer.

Looking up, he saw a swarm of flies coming at him. They smelled him from far away and couldn't resist! In a moment he was surrounded.

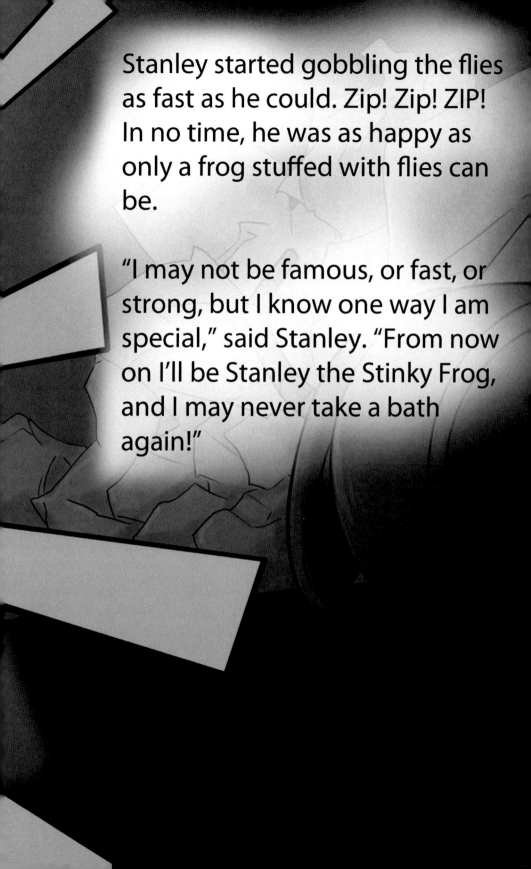

Stanley started gobbling the flies as fast as he could. Zip! Zip! ZIP! In no time, he was as happy as only a frog stuffed with flies can be.

"I may not be famous, or fast, or strong, but I know one way I am special," said Stanley. "From now on I'll be Stanley the Stinky Frog, and I may never take a bath again!"

And Stanley the Stinky Frog hopped happily home with a cloud of flies around him.

Author's Note

Thank you so much for reading all about Stanley and his slightly-smelly adventure! I hope you always remember that in everything you do you should keep working hard toward your goals (but take baths, too)! It took a lot of time, effort, and help from friends to bring Stanley and all of Frogtown to life.

So don't give up, do a little something every day, and never be afraid to ask for help.

Please look for more of Stanley and his friends coming soon!

Made in the USA
Monee, IL
24 July 2023

39417588R00029